DIARY OF AN
ICE PRINCESS

Slush Puppy Love

For Polly Rose Hill and Roberta Joy Hill

Copyright © 2020 by Christina Soontornvat

Illustrations by Barbara Szepesi Szucs, copyright © 2020 by Scholastic Inc.

All rights reserved. Published by Scholastic Inc., *Publishers since 1920.* SCHOLASTIC and associated logos are trademarks and/or registered trademarks of Scholastic Inc.

The publisher does not have any control over and does not assume any responsibility for author or third-party websites or their content.

No part of this publication may be reproduced, stored in a retrieval system, or transmitted in any form or by any means, electronic, mechanical, photocopying, recording, or otherwise, without written permission of the publisher. For information regarding permission, write to Scholastic Inc., Attention: Permissions Department, 557 Broadway, New York, NY 10012.

This book is a work of fiction. Names, characters, places, and incidents are either the product of the author's imagination or are used fictitiously, and any resemblance to actual persons, living or dead, business establishments, events, or locales is entirely coincidental.

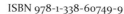

ISBN 978-1-338-60749-9

10 9 8 7 6 5 4 3 2 1   20 21 22 23 24

Printed in the U.S.A. 23

First printing 2020

Book design by Yaffa Jaskoll

DIARY OF AN
ICE PRINCESS

Slush Puppy Love

Christina Soontornvat

Illustrations by
Barbara Szepesi Szucs

SCHOLASTIC INC.

BEWARE OF BRAINSTORMS

✳ THURSDAY ✳

Dear Diary,

Today in Ms. Collier's class I learned a new word: *brainstorming*. Nope, it doesn't mean creating a storm with mind power. It means coming up with a bunch of ideas. Aren't Groundlings (also known as humans) so funny?

Our class was learning all about simple machines. Ms. Collier gave us a challenge: We had to use simple machines to move a jumbo marshmallow from one side of the classroom to the other *without* touching it at all.

If it were up to me, I would just create a blast of wintry wind to blow

the marshmallow across the room—but of course I couldn't do that. My winter magic powers are a complete secret when I'm at school with Groundlings. The only person who knows about my powers is my best friend, Claudia. Luckily that's exactly who I was partnered up with.

Our "brainstorms":

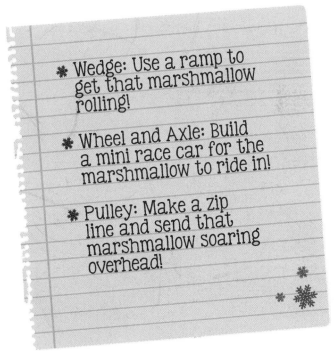

* Wedge: Use a ramp to get that marshmallow rolling!

* Wheel and Axle: Build a mini race car for the marshmallow to ride in!

* Pulley: Make a zip line and send that marshmallow soaring overhead!

We decided the pulley idea was the most fun. While we were sketching out our plan, I tried to ask Claudia some sneaky questions.

"So . . ." I began. "Our family is having game night tonight. Don't you just *love* board games?"

Claudia shrugged. "Yeah, they're fun."

"Right," I said. "But not as fun as making crafts. Don't you just *love* craft supplies?"

She looked at me funny. "Yeah, craft supplies are good . . ."

"Don't you wish you had a kit full of new craft supplies? Or beads? Don't you just *love* beads?"

Claudia put her hands on her hips.
"Lina, what is all this about?"

"Your birthday is coming up, and
I don't know what to get you!" I
blurted.

Claudia laughed. "Is that all? You

know you don't have to get me anything special."

Yes, of course I know I don't *have* to. But I want to, Diary. Claudia is my best friend, and she's the only person on Earth (literally) who knows that I'm actually an ice princess who lives in a castle in the clouds. Plus, Claudia always gets me perfect presents. This year she got me gloves knitted with conductive thread so I can still play video games even if I'm in the middle of a blizzard!

"Well, what are your parents getting you?" I asked.

"They promised me that this year I could finally get a puppy . . ."

Perfect! I'd get Claudia a collar for her new dog!

". . . but then last week we learned my dad is allergic." She sighed sadly. "The best I can hope for is a gecko."

Diary, I feel so bad for Claudia. She has always wanted a dog. Whatever

present I come up with for her needs

to be so good that she'll forget all about

wanting a puppy.

MAGICALLY MIFFED

Today after school I brainstormed a list of all the things I could get Claudia for her birthday.

This should be so easy! I thought about what cool dog-inspired gifts I would like.

My brainstorms:

* A stuffed toy dog.

* A sweatshirt with a dog on the front.

* A dog-of-the-month calendar.

But Claudia already has so many dog-themed things. None of those gifts seemed like something she would really want.

Then I heard Mom calling my name from downstairs. "Lina! I need you to come here right now, young lady!"

Anytime Mom calls me *young lady*, I know it can't be good.

Downstairs, Mom stood in the dining

room with her arms crossed. "Lina, did you leave the pitcher of lemonade out again?"

Uh-oh. I'm not supposed to leave any food or drinks out because Gusty will jump up and get into them. Sure enough, I looked down and saw him sitting in the middle of a sticky puddle with a guilty look on his face.

"Please get a towel and clean this up," said Mom. "And then give Gusty a bath."

"Okay, I will," I said.

As soon as Mom walked out of the room, Gusty started whining.

"Don't give me that look," I said. "This is all your fault. Lucky for you, I can get this cleaned up in a jiffy."

I pushed up my sleeves and held out my hands. I blew a cold breath over my fingers and pointed them at the puddle of lemonade. The sticky liquid froze into icy crystals that rose up off the floor and swirled into a frosty cloud. A lemonade cloud!

I waved my hands to send the

lemonade cloud flying out the dining room door to the courtyard.

"Easy, freezy," I said with a smile. "Now Gusty, let's get you into the bath."

A few minutes later, Gusty was enjoying his soapy bath upstairs when I heard Mom yelling again.

"LINA WINDTAMER RUDDER WINTERHEART, GET DOWN HERE RIGHT NOW, YOUNG LADY!"

Ooh, when Mom calls me a young lady *and* uses my full name, I know I'm in gigantic trouble.

I grabbed a soaking-wet Gusty and ran down to Mom's office. The lemonade cloud hovered over her desk and rained sticky drops all over her papers! I must have sent the cloud out the wrong door!

"Lina, I told you to clean up that mess!"

"I did! I cleaned it up with magic," I said.

"Lina, not every problem should be solved with magic. Your powers are getting stronger, and you need to think before you use them. You will clean this up. *With a towel this time.*"

Diary, do you know what *miffed* means? It means mad, but not super mad. Like halfway between annoyed and mad.

As I sopped up the lemonade with the towel, I was miffed at Mom. For months my family has been pushing me to get better at using my magic powers. Well, I got better! And now she wants me to stop?

Good thing tomorrow is Saturday. On

Saturdays I go to Granddad's castle.

"Granddad will understand," I grumbled.

Talk about words I never thought I'd say!

SECRETS IN THE SNOW

☀ SATURDAY ☀

Mom flies me to Granddad's castle
every Saturday for Winterheart lessons.
Every member of our royal family has
magic powers. Mom and Granddad are
both Windtamers, which means they
can control the wind and weather. I'm

a Winterheart, and Granddad has been helping me improve my powers over ice and snow.

"LINA, TODAY WE WILL PRACTICE SNOW SCULPTING," Granddad boomed. (Granddad yells when he talks. I guess when you're the North Wind, you get to do that.)

Snow sculpting is one of my favorite things to work on. I can make almost anything out of snow and ice. My favorite things to make are animals.

The best creatures to sculpt with snow:

* Snow unicorn

* Snow llama

* Snow pandasus (a panda bear with wings)

"EXCELLENT, LINA. YOUR POWERS ARE IMPROVING STEADILY. I WANT YOU TO KEEP USING YOUR MAGIC A LITTLE BIT EVERY DAY."

"Tell that to Mom," I grumbled.

Granddad raised one bushy eyebrow. **"WHAT'S GOING ON BETWEEN YOU TWO?"**

I told him all about how Mom got mad at me for cleaning up lemonade with magic. "Isn't that just so unfair?"

"YOUR MOM HAS A POINT. MAGIC CAN SOLVE PROBLEMS, BUT IT CAN ALSO CAUSE TROUBLE."

I huffed. "Not if you know what you're doing."

"YOUR GREAT-AUNT SUNDER KNEW WHAT SHE WAS DOING, AND LOOK WHAT HAPPENED TO HER."

"What do you mean? What happened to her?"

Granddad started to answer, but then changed the subject. **"WOW, I AM FEELING THE NEED FOR A SNACK. HOW ABOUT YOU? I'LL MAKE US SOME ANTS IN A FOG!"**

Diary, Granddad volunteering to spread peanut butter and raisins on marshmallows is a sure sign that he's trying to avoid me.

No one in our family likes to talk about Granddad's sister, Great-Aunt Sunder. I always thought she was just grumpy or something. But the funny way Granddad was acting meant there had to be more to the story.

And I was determined to figure out what it was.

ALL IN THE FAMILY

After Winterheart practice, Granddad usually takes a nap in the afternoon. (Diary, when the North Wind snores, it can shake the whole room!)

Usually that's the most boring part of my visit, but today I couldn't wait for him to fall asleep. As soon as I heard alls rumbling, I crept down the allway to the library.

Granddad's library is amazing. He has hundreds of ancient books about all kinds of magic. I walked up and down the bookshelves looking for something—anything—about my great-aunt Sunder. Finally, I found a dusty, old book that looked promising.

A chill crept up my spine. I had no idea that Great-Aunt Sunder is a Winterheart just like me. According to the book, she used to live with her brothers and sisters in the skies. Her powers grew and grew until she had become the most powerful of all the Four Winds.

Wow, Diary, does that mean she was even more powerful than Granddad?

The book said that Sunder began to use magic in ways no one ever had before. She created ice mountains and winter cyclones. She even made snow beasts. She sculpted animals from snow and blew magic over them to bring them to life.

Her brothers and sisters were scared of her powers. She had to move away from them, all the way to the South Pole.

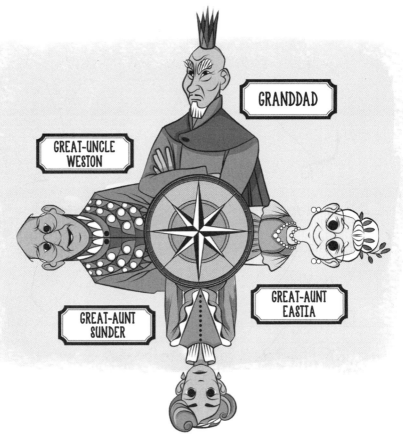

GRANDDAD

GREAT-UNCLE WESTON

GREAT-AUNT EASTIA

GREAT-AUNT SUNDER

Does that mean Great-Aunt Sunder got cast out of our family? Just because she made some animals out of snow? That doesn't seem fair!

I wanted to read more, but I heard Granddad start to wake up. I quickly shut the book and put it back on the shelf.

"Did you have a good nap, Granddad?" I asked as he came into the library.

"I WAS JUST RESTING MY EYES! GOOD WORK TODAY, LINA. I THINK YOU LEARNED SOME THINGS."

Wow, Diary, he had no idea.

5

THE PROBLEM WITH PRESENTS

As interesting as it was to learn about my family secrets, I sort of forgot about it. I mean, I had really important things on my mind.

To get my thoughts in order, I decided to make a list.

Things on my mind:

❋ What sport is better,
roller-skating or
ice-skating?

❋ Should I ask Mom to let
me cut my bangs?

❋ How can I convince Dad
to stop packing beans
in my lunch?

Most important of all: What in the world am I going to get Claudia for her birthday? Her party is in one week, and I have zero ideas!

I tried brainstorming another list. I tried searching through my toys for

inspiration. I even tried stomping as hard as I could down the castle stairs.

(Stomping didn't really help me come up with any ideas. It just felt good.)

Nothing I came up with seemed good enough for my best friend. Finally I had no choice but to go into the living room and flop down onto the floor at my parents' feet.

"It's no good!" I moaned. "I have no idea what to get Claudia for her birthday."

"You're so creative," said Dad. "You should make her something."

"Oh, that's a great suggestion,"

added Mom. "You could make her a card. Ooh! Or how about a puppet?"

"Mom, Claudia doesn't want a card or a puppet!"

"What does she want, then?" Mom asked.

I sighed. "What she really wants is a puppy, and it's not like I can make a—"

Oh, Diary.

My brain stormed so hard that it started a hurricane inside my skull.

I raced up the stairs. "Mom, Dad, I'm going up to my room now!"

"Everything okay, honey?"

"Yup, just fine! I'm going to go and . . . make a puppet!"

LIKE SNOWBODY'S BUSINESS

On my way up the stairs, I scooped Gusty into my arms. He barked excitedly.

"*Shh*, buddy. I'm going to need you to be super cooperative right now, okay?"

I set him down in my room and closed the door behind us.

"Okay, Gusty, you're going to be my model. So strike a pose."

I kept my eyes on Gusty as I held out my arms and wiggled my fingers. I waved my hands over the falling snowflakes, sculpting them into shape. When I was done, I was pretty proud of myself. My snow puppy looked great!

Next came the hard part: breathing life into the snow sculpture. The book in Granddad's library said that Great-Aunt Sunder blew a "magical breath" onto her snow beasts. I had no idea what that was like, but I shut my eyes and tried my best to copy the pose in the illustration.

I put my lips together like a whistle

and blew a cool puff of air onto the
snow puppy. Nothing happened. I blew
again, harder this time. And then I did
some extra blowing for good measure.
I waved my fingers over the puppy. I
shut my eyes really hard. I wiggled my
bottom (because hey, why not, right?).

When I heard Gusty yipping, I opened my eyes.

At first, the snow puppy didn't look any different. But then the snow sparkled. And then . . . it moved. I leaned in closer to the snow puppy.

It licked my face!

And then it hopped onto my lap!

Oh. My. Blizzards.

Diary, I made a snow beastie!

BEST IN SNOW

Diary, it is a miracle that I made it all the way down to Claudia's house in my dad's airplane without him finding out I had a *dog* in my backpack!

Dad is a Groundling, so he can't fly through the sky on a gust of wind like

Mom can. Thank goodness the motor on his plane is super noisy. It drowned out the sounds of the puppy's sniffing and panting.

"What did you end up making Claudia for her present?" Dad called from the front seat.

"A puppy . . . I mean a puppet! A puppy puppet!" I had hidden the backpack on the floor beside my seat. The snow puppy kept trying to get out of it, and I had to keep feeding her ice cubes to keep her still. She had so much energy I worried she would jump right out of my backpack!

Dad dropped me off in front of
Claudia's house. I rang the doorbell, and
she answered it. "Oh hi, Lina! What are
you doing here?"

The backpack on my shoulders
wiggled and wriggled. "Um, I'm here to
give you your birthday present early. As
in, immediately!"

My backpack whimpered.

"Let's go to your room!" I grabbed Claudia's hand and pulled her up the stairs.

In her room, I opened the backpack, and a ball of white fur tumbled out.

Claudia gasped. "Lina! Is *that* my present?"

"Happy birthday?"

"But what about my dad? His allergies . . ."

"I don't think it will be a problem because she's not a real dog. She's a snow dog. As in, *made* of snow."

Right then the snow puppy hopped up and licked Claudia's face.

I laughed. "She's super energetic. I think it's because I breathed a lot of life into her."

"What are you talking about?" asked Claudia.

"I'll explain everything later. But first, you should give her a name."

The puppy licked Claudia's face again, and she giggled. "She's like a fluffy, flurry puff of snow! Oh!" Claudia looked up at me. "That's what I should name her—Flurry!"

When the puppy heard her new name, she leaped up and gave a happy yip.

"So what do you think?" I asked. "Do you like her?"

"Are you kidding?" Claudia threw her arms around my neck. "Lina, this is the best birthday present ever!"

8

PUPPY PLAYDATE

☀ TUESDAY ☀

At first, Claudia's parents were not
exactly thrilled that I gave her a dog
as an early birthday gift. But when they
saw how excited she was—and when
they learned that Flurry would not make
her dad sneeze—they gave in.

Claudia and I decided not to tell our parents where Flurry actually came from. There is a saying that goes: "Ignorance is bliss." It means that you can't worry about something if you don't know about it.

Besides, what is there to worry about? Claudia loves her new puppy, and that's all that matters!

Today after school, she brought Flurry up to our castle for a puppy playdate with Gusty. The two pups chased each other through the clouds in front of our castle. Flurry is so fluffy and white that she looked like one of the clouds!

"Aw, Gusty is so happy to have a little friend," I said.

"I'm just glad Flurry has someone else to play with," said Claudia. "You said she was a bundle of energy, and you were right. She's wearing me out!"

"Well, this is perfect, then. Our dogs

can have a playdate, and we can have one too!"

While Gusty and Flurry chased each other, Claudia and I played hide-and-seek in the clouds. After a few rounds, we went to check on our puppies. We found Gusty resting on a cloud tuft, but Flurry was nowhere to be seen.

"She must have run into the castle," I said. "Let's go find her!"

"Flurry!" called Claudia. "She does this at my house too. Yesterday she went missing, and I found her in the yard chewing up our garden hose!"

We searched all over the castle: down in the kitchen, up in the throne room, my dad's hangar where he keeps his airplanes. I was starting to get a little worried, Diary, because a castle in the clouds isn't exactly the safest place for a puppy to go wandering. If she ran too far, she might run right off our magical clouds, and . . .

Oh gosh, I didn't want to think about it!

Ruff, ruff, ruff!

"That's her!" said Claudia.

We followed the barking sounds to my parents' room and into their closet.

Diary, it was a complete mess! Flurry had gotten into my mom's trunk and pulled out her nicest ball gowns. Beaded dresses and satin ribbons were strewn all over the place!

"Oh no," said Claudia.

"Oh double no," I said.

Flurry had one of my mom's favorite silk shoes in her teeth. "Drop it, girl," I pleaded.

"She loves chewing shoes," said

Claudia. "You better get it from her before she rips it to shreds!"

I held out one hand and, with a wave of my fingers, formed an ice treat in the shape of a dog bone. "Come get it, Flurry!"

Instantly, Flurry dropped the shoe and bounded over, slurping the ice bone up from my hand.

"See, she was hungry," I said, petting

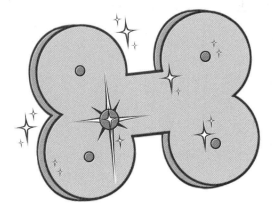

Flurry's head. "She just needs some puppy training."

"Well, it's a good thing she likes ice," said Claudia. "We have a whole freezer full of ice cubes at home."

I made Flurry more icy treats to munch on while Claudia and I packed Mom's gowns back into her trunk. As long as Flurry was munching on ice, she was perfectly chilled out.

See, Diary? Mom was totally wrong when she said magic can't solve every problem!

9

PUPPY TRAINING

✳ WEDNESDAY ✳

This morning I was just about to walk into our school building when Claudia leaped out of the bushes and grabbed my sleeve.

"You scared me!" I said. "What are you doing hiding in the bushes?"

"I've got a big problem," said Claudia. "Look!"

She pulled me around the corner. There was Flurry, panting and running in circles.

"She followed me to school!" said Claudia. "I don't know what to do. She won't listen to a word I say!"

Flurry yipped happily and came bounding toward me. She knocked me over backward into the bush. "Oh my glaciers, Flurry, you are getting so big!"

"That's another problem," said Claudia. "She's getting huge! I would just pick her up and carry her home, but I can't lift her all by myself anymore."

"How about ice treats?" I asked.

"I ran out of them!" said Claudia. "Please help me get her home, Lina. You're the closest thing to an ice machine around here!"

We had about ten minutes before the school bell rang. Claudia lives really close to the school, but we would still have to hurry.

I made sure no one could see us, then swirled my fingers over my palm to make ice treats. I held one out to Flurry as I walked down the sidewalk. "Come on, girl, come on!"

With a bark, she hopped up and followed me. We held the treats out to her, coaxing her all the way back to Claudia's house. Finally we were able to get her into the backyard and shut the gate.

We ran as fast as we could back to school and got inside the door just after the bell rang.

TARDY SLIP

NAME: _____ TIME IN: _____

DATE: _____

CLASS: _____

REASON: _____

_____

EXCUSED: ☐ UNEXCUSED: ☐ STAFF: _____

Claudia looked on the verge of tears as we walked to the principal's office to fill out our late forms. "I've never gotten a tardy slip before!" she whispered.

As we trudged to Ms. Collier's class with our tardy slips in hand, I wondered if Claudia still thought that Flurry was the best present ever.

ALL THAT GLITTERS IS COLD

☀ FRIDAY ☀

Tonight at dinner, we were served yellow noodle soup. My favorite.

We drank lychee soda. Also my favorite.

And for dessert?

Mango-and-whipped-cloud pudding. My favorite of all favorites.

"Mom?" I asked. "What's going on? Do you have to leave on a business trip or something?"

She smiled. "No, sweetie. I just wanted to apologize for being so tough on you the other day. You know, when I said that you can't solve every problem with magic."

"It's okay, Mom. Really."

"I just worry about anyone in our family letting their magic get out of hand," said Mom. "Especially after what happened with your great-aunt Sunder."

My ears perked up. This was my

chance to learn more about my

mysterious relative.

"I was reading about her in

Granddad's library," I said. "I don't

think it's fair that she got banished to

the South Pole just because she became

powerful."

"Banished?" Mom shook her head.

"No, that isn't what happened. She left on her own. Sunder wanted to use her powers to do everything. Even when her magic caused problems, she wouldn't stop. She and your granddad argued, and then she packed up and moved down to the South Pole."

"That's terrible. They're supposed to be family."

Mom squeezed my hand. "Families can be . . . complicated. Granddad still loves Sunder, but he also felt she was being reckless with her magic. Lina, having magic powers is a big responsibility. We all have to take it seriously. Do you understand?"

I nodded and told her I understood.

But actually, I feel pretty confused.

Diary, Mom said Great-Aunt Sunder's

magic caused problems. Part of me wants

to know what those problems were.

The other part of me is way too

scared to ask.

THE TRUTH COMES OUT

Diary, I'm not so sure if ignorance really is bliss. I didn't want to worry about Great-Aunt Sunder's magic, but finally I decided that I had to find out the truth.

This morning was Saturday, so, as usual,

we went to Granddad's for Winterheart practice. Also as usual, Granddad took his afternoon nap.

As soon as he was snoring away, I crept back into his library to find the book about Great-Aunt Sunder. I turned to the chapter I had been reading about the snow beasts. I flipped the page and read all about what had really happened.

It was just like Mom said. Great-Aunt Sunder let her magic go too far. And now I had done the exact same thing! I had made a snow beast (well, okay, just a wee beastie) and brought it to life. Even worse, I had fed Flurry ice treats

Sunder fed ice to her magical creatures, and they grew to tremendous size. The beasts became powerful and dangerous. Snow serpents sank ships in the northern seas. Great snow bears prowled the mountains. The more ice the creatures ate, the larger they grew, until finally Sunder's siblings, the North, East, and West Winds, had to use all their powers to stop the beasts.

to keep her calm, but they were just making her grow!

I rushed to the phone on Granddad's desk and called Claudia.

"Claudia?" I said when she answered. "Listen, there's a problem with Flurry–"

"No kidding!" Claudia interrupted. "I keep feeding her ice cubes, but she's still so hyper! She's wrecking the house, and my parents are–"

I heard a loud CRASH on the other end of the phone.

"Uh-oh!" said Claudia. "I gotta go!"

"Wait!"

But Claudia had already hung up. I

didn't get a chance to tell her not to feed Flurry any more ice cubes.

Ignorance is definitely not bliss in this case! Claudia needs to know about the problem with Flurry—and fast!

LO AND BE COLD

When Dad came and picked me up in his plane, I immediately asked him to drop me off at Claudia's house.

When Claudia opened the front door, she looked exhausted.

"Where's Flurry?" I asked.

"In the backyard," said Claudia with

a yawn. "I finally got her to sit down. I think she wore herself out from all the jumping around. She broke our trampoline!"

My jaw dropped. "She *broke* it? What did your parents say?"

"They're out running errands. They left me with my brother, who thankfully wears his headphones when he's coding on his computer. I don't think he's heard anything that's been going on."

"Okay, don't worry," I said. "I'm sure we can fix this before your parents get home. Whatever you do, don't feed her any more ice cubes! It will just make her grow bigger."

Claudia nodded to the window that looked onto her backyard. "Yeah, I think I may have figured that out on my own."

When I looked outside, I couldn't believe it. Flurry was the size of a small pony!

Claudia's brother, Jaiden, peeked his head out of his room. He looked out the window too. "Claudia, what have you been feeding that dog?"

"Um, ice cubes?"

Jaiden shook his head. "Mom and Dad said you could have a puppy. Not a llama."

Claudia glared at him. "Jaiden, don't you have code to write or something?"

Jaiden shrugged his shoulders, put his headphones back on, and retreated to his room. Claudia and I whispered about what to do.

"As annoying as my brother is, he's right," said Claudia. "My mom and dad are never going to let me keep Flurry if she gets any bigger!"

"It's okay; everything will be fine," I said. "I'm sure we can figure out a way to fix this."

"Lina, that's what you said about the ice cubes—and they just made things worse!"

Suddenly we heard a huge crash outside. We rushed out to the backyard.

Claudia gulped. "Tell me what you were saying again about everything being fine."

Oh Diary. Where Claudia's fence used to be was a huge, gaping hole.

Flurry was nowhere to be seen.

13

CREATURE SIGHTING

Claudia and I ran out through the hole in the fence. We looked up and down her street, but we didn't see Flurry anywhere.

Diary, my heart was pounding so hard. I started to realize what I had done. I had used my Winterheart powers to make a magical creature. I had brought it to life. And now it was running wild!

What if my family found out? What if they were so mad that they banished me to go live at the South Pole with Great-Aunt Sunder? What if I never got to see Claudia or my parents ever again?

We had to find that dog.

"Flurry!" I shouted.

"What if she runs into a busy street?" asked Claudia.

"Don't worry; I'm sure a car would stop before it hit her."

"I'm not worried about her. I'm worried about the car!"

We ran up and down Claudia's block, but we didn't see any sign of Flurry, and we couldn't hear her barking.

An older woman who lived next door to Claudia was working in her garden.

"Excuse me, Ms. Flores," said Claudia. "Have you seen my dog run by here?"

"I'm sorry, I haven't seen a dog," said the neighbor. "But I did see a fluffy llama galloping by."

Claudia and I looked at each other. A fluffy llama? That had to be Flurry!

"Which way did the llama, er, gallop?" I asked.

Ms. Flores pointed up the street.

Claudia smacked one hand to her forehead. "Of course! She's going to the school! She knows the way from following me. Come on, bikes will be faster. You can ride my brother's."

Claudia turned back to her house to get the bicycles.

I pulled Claudia to a stop. "I don't know how to ride a bike. I don't have one up in the clouds."

Diary, this is why it's great to have Claudia for a best friend. Because she

doesn't let something like "I don't know how to ride a bike" stop her.

"You sit on the handlebars, and I'll pump the pedals. Let's go!"

14

PUPPY-SIZE PROBLEMS

✳ SATURDAY ✳

Diary, I have ridden through the skies
on the wind. I have peered down at
the world from the tops of clouds.
And never—never—have I experienced
anything more terrifying than sitting on

the handlebars of my best friend's bike
while she pedaled us downhill.

It was awesome.

When Claudia pulled up in front
of the school, the whole building was
quiet. The front doors were locked, of
course, because it was Sunday. I peered

in through the windows. It was weird seeing my usually busy school building completely empty with all the lights off.

"Flurry!" called Claudia. "Gosh, I hope my hunch was right and she came here. Otherwise I don't know if my legs have the strength to bike us anywhere else!"

Suddenly we heard barking coming from the other side of the building. We ran around to the playground at the back of the school.

There was Flurry, bounding from one side of the playground to the other. She ran up to the top of the slide and slid down on her tummy, then ran up to the

top to do it again. But she was so big
that the slide was bending under her
weight!

"Oh no!" said Claudia. "Flurry's going
to break the slide!"

I looked over both shoulders to make
sure no one was around to see. Then I
held up my hands and began creating

long strands of ice. Moving my fingers, I wove the ice into thick ropes that I strung across the top of the slide. I thought the barrier would stop her from going down.

Instead, Flurry chomped a huge bite right out of the ice ropes and slurped them up like noodles! With every bite she grew bigger and bigger and bigger . . .

Flurry launched herself down the slide, and this time the metal sagged under her weight and broke in half. Flurry tumbled to the ground, but she was so big that the fall didn't seem to bother her one bit.

"Flurry, SIT!" Claudia shouted.

The ground shook as Flurry plopped down in front of us. Diary, she was now as big as a full-grown horse. She may have been a giant, but she was still an adorable giant. Huge puddles of drool pooled at her feet as she panted happily.

"Good girl," said Claudia, approaching Flurry slowly. "Just stay calm . . . stay sitting." Flurry let Claudia pet her behind the ears. I was sure that this giant, sweet puppy would be done with all the running around.

But I guess puppies don't stay still for long. She jumped up and bounded straight for the back doors of the school.

"Flurry, stop!" we shouted.

But she didn't stop, and now that she was even bigger, the back door didn't stand a chance. She busted it down and ran inside!

I raised my arms to create an ice barrier, but then I lowered them. If Flurry ate any more ice, she would be as big as a house!

Now I understood why Granddad and Great-Aunt Sunder had argued. Magic could get out of hand if you weren't careful.

I wasn't going to be like Great-Aunt Sunder. I knew I could figure out a way to solve this problem without using magic. I just had to *think*.

Through the school windows, we could see Flurry running down the halls and into classrooms. She knocked over desks and slobbered on bulletin boards.

"She'd better not find our classroom," said Claudia in horror. "If she ruins our simple machines project, I'm going to be so mad at her!"

Simple machines.

I grabbed Claudia by the arm. "Come on!"

"What? Where are we going?"

"To the gym! My brain has stormed!"

A SIMPLE SOLUTION

Our PE teacher keeps a closet in the gym stocked with all the sports equipment you could ever dream of.

I swung open the doors and started looking. "Climbing rope! Perfect. Now where is that parachute . . . ?"

"What are you doing?" asked Claudia as I piled her arms high with coils of rope.

"I can't use magic to stop Flurry from wrecking the school. So we're going to have to use something else. We need to build a trap. A gigantic puppy trap."

"A trap?" asked Claudia with a shocked look.

"Don't worry; it won't hurt her, I promise. It'll just slow her down. Let's get all this stuff outside."

Back on the playground, we spread out the gigantic, colorful parachute under a big oak tree. I strung the rope through the outer loops of the parachute.

I handed the end of the climbing rope
to Claudia. "Hold this for a minute." I
held out my hands and focused my ice-
making powers.

"But I thought you said we had to stop
Flurry *without* using magic," said Claudia.

"Well, maybe just a smidgen of magic,"

I said, forming a ball of ice in my hands. I swirled it around and around until the ice had made a frozen wheel with a groove down the middle.

Claudia beamed. "A pulley! Lina, that's perfect!"

I threaded the climbing rope through the ice pulley. "When Flurry gets out onto the middle of the parachute, we'll just pull down on the rope, and she'll get scooped up."

Just then we saw Flurry through the windows, crashing into one of the first-grade classrooms.

My shoulders sagged. "I just realized that this isn't going to work."

"Why not?"

"Because Flurry is so big. She's got to weigh more than both of us put together. We'll never be able to lift her off the ground."

Claudia snapped her fingers. "Lina, how many ice pulleys can you make?"

"A lot—why?"

"Remember what Ms. Collier taught

us? You can use lots of pulleys together to make the lifting easier."

I gasped. "Mechanical advantage! I totally forgot about it. We'll have to pull longer on the rope, but we won't have to pull as hard."

We heard Flurry crash into the art room and what sounded like paintbrushes and paints scattering everywhere.

"We are going to need every advantage we can get," said Claudia. "You make the pulleys, and I'll get my bike!"

16

PULLEY-ING FOR YOU

We had the parachute in place.

We had four pulleys attached to the parachute, and four hanging from the tree branch overhead.

We had the end of the rope tied onto Claudia's bike.

We just needed one gigantic, magical
puppy dog.

"Okay, here goes nothing," I said to
Claudia. Our nearly-no-magic solution
just needed a teensy bit more magic to
make it work. I twirled my hands over

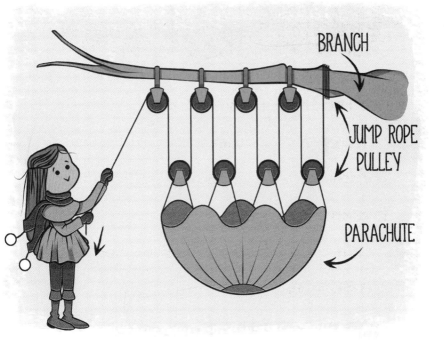

BRANCH

JUMP ROPE
PULLEY

PARACHUTE

the parachute and made a pile of bone-shaped ice treats. "Oh, Flurry!" I called. "Got some tasty treats for you! Come and get 'em!"

We heard some happy barking and then the scrabble of paws running across the floor.

"Okay, get ready!" I called to Claudia.

A huge ball of white fur burst out through the gym doors and rushed to the center of the parachute. Flurry happily started slurping up the ice treats.

"Pedal!" I shouted to Claudia.

She put the pedal to the metal and raced across the field on her bike.

The rope tightened, and the parachute cinched up around Flurry like a gigantic, colorful dumpling wrapper. Claudia strained on the bike as Flurry lifted off the ground. I ran out to Claudia and pushed her from behind. We grunted and sweated, but finally we managed to hoist that dog into the air.

We tied the rope to another tree so Flurry couldn't escape.

Claudia looked worried. "Do you think she's okay in there? I feel so bad tying her up like that."

We walked up to the parachute swinging from the tree branch.

We heard sniffling and panting

coming from inside. A few minutes later, we heard the loud rumble of dog snores. Diary, she fell asleep! I guess all that running around had really tired her out.

Talk about tired. Claudia and I high-fived in celebration, and then

immediately collapsed on the ground. We were completely wiped!

"Now what?" asked Claudia.

I sighed. "As much as I hate to do this, I think it's time to call in some Windtamer reinforcements."

17

THE LOOK

Diary, there are several levels of being in trouble in my family.

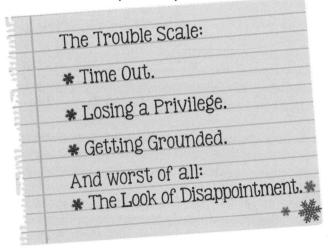

The Trouble Scale:

* Time Out.

* Losing a Privilege.

* Getting Grounded.

And worst of all:
* The Look of Disappointment.

After Mom and Granddad swooped down to our school to help us, we all flew back up to Granddad's castle with Flurry in tow. Both he and Mom stood over Claudia and me, giving us double Looks of Disappointment.

It was super intense.

I broke down and told them the entire story of how I had created Flurry and given her to Claudia, all about the ice treats, and how Flurry had wrecked the school. By the time I finished, I was nearly in tears.

"I'm so sorry," I told them. "I will definitely never use my magic to do something like that again. So please

don't banish me to the South Pole! I
want to stay in the family!"

Mom and Granddad dropped their
looks and hugged me close.

"Of course we aren't going to banish
you, silly," said Mom, smoothing my

hair. "You're in this family forever, no matter what."

"**NOW YOU UNDERSTAND THAT MAGIC HAS ITS LIMITS, LINA,**" Granddad said. "**OF EVERYTHING YOU HAVE LEARNED, THAT MAY BE THE MOST IMPORTANT LESSON OF ALL.**"

Mom squeezed my shoulder. "But you do still have to make things right. You and Claudia will go back to your school and clean everything up. With trash bags and gloves, not magic."

Claudia and I both saluted. Trash pickup was a thousand times better than the Look of Disappointment.

"But what about Flurry?" I asked. "Is she going back to Claudia's house?"

Claudia shook her head. "Flurry is so sweet, but I had no idea that a puppy was so hard to take care of. Especially one that's the size of a golf cart."

"FLURRY CAN STAY UP HERE WITH ME," said Granddad. "THERE'S PLENTY OF ROOM FOR HER TO BOUNCE AROUND, AND YOU BOTH CAN COME VISIT HER WHENEVER YOU WANT. BUT I'M PUTTING HER ON A STRICT NO-ICE REGIMEN. FROM NOW ON, IT'S ONLY ANTS IN A FOG."

He got a double hug from me and Claudia for that!

18

A BIRTHDAY TO REMEMBER

Today was Claudia's birthday party. Her house and backyard were full of friends and family. Claudia's parents had fixed her trampoline and packed it with colorful balloons. There were tables laid out with all sorts of yummy food.

Claudia's brother, Jaiden, had even set aside his computer to come out and join in the fun.

When Claudia saw me, she ran to give me a hug. "My parents bought me a pet for my birthday! You have to come meet Cuddles!"

"Wait, they got you a puppy?"

Claudia shook her head. "After Flurry, I think I might wait awhile to get a dog. I decided I need a more chilled-out pet."

In Claudia's room was a big glass tank. Inside, a peach-colored gecko flicked out his tongue at me. He was really cute! "Cuddles looks pretty chill to me."

"And I can still go visit Flurry at your granddad's place whenever I need some puppy time," said Claudia. "Speaking of Flurry, how is she doing?"

"Great. She loves ants in a fog. And I think Granddad likes having the company. He plays fetch with her in the morning, and then they take naps together in the afternoon. You should hear them snoring—they sound like a thunderstorm!"

After cake it was time for presents. I handed Claudia the box that I'd brought with me. "I made it myself," I told her.

As she started to open it, Claudia paused and gave me a look. "This isn't a barking ball of fluff that's going to lick my face, is it?"

I laughed. "It's not going to lick your face, but there may be some fluffiness involved."

Claudia opened the box and looked inside. "Oh, Lina, these are perfect. I love them!"

Make a Snow Beastie

YOU WILL NEED:

* Ice cubes
* Blender (Ask a grown-up to help you operate it!)
* Spoon
* Plate for your beastie
* Paper towels for cleanup
* Optional: Googly eyes, paper or fabric cut into the shapes of ears, noses, etc.
* Always ask a grown-up for permission before you get started!

MAKE SOME "SNOW"

First, make sure you have a clean, dry workspace. You may want to cover your surface with paper towels or a plastic tablecloth to protect it. Any spills can be cleaned up with soap and water.

Transfer the ice cubes from the freezer to the blender. Making "snow" works best if you use dry ice cubes that haven't had the chance to start melting. Have an adult blend the ice into a fine powder using the highest setting on your blender. Don't overblend, or the snow will turn mushy!

SCULPT YOUR SNOW BEASTS

Working quickly, use a spoon to scoop some "snow" onto a plate. Sculpt the snow using your hands or tools you find around the kitchen, like measuring cups or spatulas. As the snow melts, the liquid water will cause the solid ice to stick together, allowing you to form simple shapes. Try making a snow puppy, a kitten,

or even a panda! If you like, you can use googly eyes or fabric or paper shapes to add some features to your wee beastie.

To save your beastie from melting, stick it in the freezer. With enough ice, you can create an entire zoo of snow creatures!

Be cool—not warm—and read a sneak peek of Lina's next adventure!

DIARY OF AN
ICE PRINCESS

Icing on the Snowflake

Christina Soontornvat

📚SCHOLASTIC

TO HAVE AND TO COLD

* SATURDAY *

Dear Diary,

Not having any brothers or sisters can get lonely sometimes. But lucky for me, I have a ton of cousins to make up for it! I love all my cousins so much.

But if I had to pick one cousin I wish I could be like when I get older, it would be Wendy. I have always looked up to

Wendy. Like everyone in my family, she has magical weather powers.

She used to babysit me when I was little, and we had the best time playing together. The thing I love most about her is that even though she is also a royal princess, she likes being silly and isn't afraid to get messy.

I never thought someone could be cooler than Wendy. But I was wrong. Because her boyfriend, Sunny, is just as awesome.

Ahem, I mean her *fiancé*, Sunny.

Diary, I am so excited that Wendy and Sunny are getting married! I hope

one day they have adorable babies
and then *I* will get to be the cool older
cousin who babysits.

Claudia was up at our castle having a
playdate today when Wendy, Sunny, and
my Great-Aunt Eastia flew in. In our
family, it's tradition for the bride and
groom to deliver wedding invitations by
hand just before the big ceremony.

"Claudia, you and Lina are getting so
big!" said Wendy, giving us hugs. "What
happened to the little girls I used to
babysit?"

"At least Gusty is still tiny," said

Sunny as my puppy covered him in slobbery kisses.

My mom offered to take Great-Aunt Eastia's coat. "Won't you stay and have tea with us?" she asked.

"I'm afraid we don't have time," said Eastia. "We are delivering invitations all over the sky today, and we still have quite a few left."

"We have been flying all morning," Wendy whispered to me. "I need a snack or I'm going to evaporate!"

Eastia cleared her throat and scowled. I love my great-aunt, but she is also very strict about manners.

CHRISTINA SOONTORNVAT grew up behind the counter of her parents' Thai restaurant, reading stories. These days she loves to make up her own, especially if they involve magic. Christina also loves science and worked in a science museum for years before pursuing her dream of being an author. She still enjoys cooking up science experiments at home with her two young daughters. You can learn more about Christina and her books on her website at soontornvat.com.

Princess Tabby is no scaredy-cat!

Who says princesses have to be perfect?

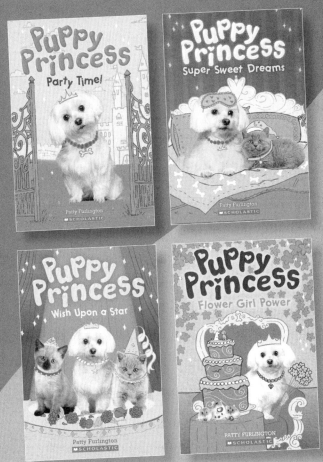

Join Princess Rosie and Cleo the kitten as they go on fun adventures around Petrovia!

scholastic.com

PUPPYPRINCESS

Oh my glaciers, Diary!

Princess Lina is the *coolest* girl in school!

scholastic.com